Simply fantastic

AN INTRODUCTION TO CLASSICAL MUSIC

Music selection and explanatory notes ANA GERHARD
Illustrations CLAUDIA LEGNAZZI

Simply fantastic

Since the beginning of time, gnomes, fairies, witches, pixies, elves, magicians and many other imaginary beings have been stirring the imaginations of children... and even their parents and grandparents! People everywhere believed that creatures dwelling in forests, caves, deserts, mountains, rivers and ponds—not to mention towns and hamlets—could move freely between the physical world and the imagination, perhaps as a reminder of reality's many dimensions.

Some of these beings are remarkably similar to humans while others resemble animals or are curious hybrids of the two. Mythical creatures may be beautiful or hideous, comical or loathsome.

From one generation to the next since time immemorial these creatures have evoked admiration, dread and sympathy. They have helped us to explain the unfathomable mysteries one's existence, confront our fears and overcome our problems. While they may occasionally give us nightmares, for the most part they help us face the world.

Perhaps this is what has inspired so many composers throughout history to depict mythical creatures in music; their works make supernatural beings more tangible and bring them to life, that we might reach out and touch them with one's imagination.

This book introduces musical compositions inspired by ancient legends, old superstitions or classic fairy tales. Their composers bring mythical creatures to life through a single instrument, a choir or a full orchestra. You will discover music that imitates the sound of voices, laughing, footsteps or movement—always for the purpose of conjuring an atmosphere that evokes the presence of these fascinating beings.

1 The Fairy-Queen

Fairies are tiny luminous creatures imagined as exceptionally beautiful women found deep in the forest among ancient trees and by babbling brooks. They are said to have descended from rebel angels, who, after being chased from Heaven, took refuge in caves, hills and rivers. Their troubled ancestry may account for the impish nature of fairies.

The plot of *The Fairy-Queen* unfolds one night in an enchanted forest where several characters from the real world encounter citizens of an imaginary realm, including Oberon and Titania, King and Queen of the Fairies.

After arguing with her husband, Oberon, Titania allows herself to be diverted by the fairies, who try to dance and sing her to sleep. The scene is entitled *Solo, Chorus and Dance of Fairies*.

Sing while we trip it on the Green;
But no ill Vapours rise or fall,
Nothing offend our Fairy Queen.

The Fairy-Queen is a masque by Henry Purcell based on William Shakespeare's comedy *A Midsummer Night's Dream*, written around 1595.

A Midsummer Night's Dream

2

A Midsummer Night's Dream
(Felix Mendelssohn)
Scherzo from the orchestral suite

This work features fairies and elves—magical creatures that resemble humans but, are much smaller and sometimes of a strange hue, such as green, red or blue. They have a reputation for playing mischievous tricks, which explains why they often get blamed when something disappears.

When Felix Mendelssohn read *A Midsummer Night's Dream* at the age of 17, he was so impressed that, in just a few days, he wrote an overture inspired by the play, expressing the beauty and poesy of William Shakespeare's imaginary realm. From the first performance, the public was struck by the work's perfection and immediately acclaimed it a masterpiece.

Seventeen years later, at the request of King Frederick William IV of Prussia, Mendelssohn composed incidental music for a ballet based on the same work, which proved every bit as successful. The scherzo included here comes from the beginning of the second act of the ballet and transports the listener into Shakespeare's magical world.

3 Puck's Dance

Preludes (Claude Debussy)
Prelude for piano

Drawn from the folklore of the British Isles, Puck is an extremely mischievous elf and trickster who appears in Shakespeare's comedy *A Midsummer Night's Dream* as King Oberon's page. The play recounts the series of eventful misunderstandings that ensue after Puck places a love potion on the eyelids of the wrong person. He also maliciously applies some potion to the eyes of Queen Titania, causing her to fall in love (to great comic effect) with a donkey!

Claude Debussy's *Preludes* reflect the composer's personal tastes as well as his favourite reading material, characters and places. The prelude entitled *Puck's Dance* depicts an affable but unpredictable character.

4 Dance of the Sugar Plum Fairy

The Nutcracker (Pyotr Ilych Tchaikovsky)
Ballet suite

The Sugar Plum Fairy is the enchanting queen of the Land of Sweets in a ballet called *The Nutcracker*. On Christmas Eve, Clara receives a nutcracker in the shape of a soldier as a gift. She is delighted with her present, but her jealous brother breaks it. When Clara falls asleep, her godfather repairs the nutcracker, which then comes to life to defend Clara against the Mouse King and his army. Afterwards, the nutcracker turns into a prince and accompanies Clara to the Land of Sweets, where they are welcomed by the Sugar Plum Fairy dancing the exquisite ballet included here.

Tchaikovsky presented *The Nutcracker* for the first time in December 1892, and it remains one of the most popular ballets of all time. The story is based on a tale entitled *The Nutcracker and the Mouse King* by E. T. A. Hoffmann.

5 The Witch Baba Yaga

Album for the Young (Pyotr Ilych Tchaikovsky)
For piano

Baba Yaga is an ugly old woman with a wrinkled, bony face, a long, bluish nose, and iron teeth for eating little children. A typical figure of Russian folklore, this witch is known throughout the world, for she is simply the Slavic version of the terrifying figures parents everywhere invoke to convince children to behave.

Known in his tender youth as the "porcelain child," Tchaikovsky included Baba Yaga in his *Album for the Young* so that young ones might overcome their fear of her through playing the piano.

Album for the Young is a collection of short pieces with titles geared to children, that Tchaikovsky composed to make learning the piano enjoyable. He drew the idea from a work of the same name by Robert Schumann, one of Tchaikovsky's favourite composers.

6 The Hut on Fowl's Legs

Pictures at an Exhibition (Modest Mussorgsky)
Orchestral suite

According to Russian folklore, the hut on fowl's legs is the abode of the wicked witch Baba Yaga. Built on two enormous chicken legs, this horrible house with walls built of human bones can move around as it pleases. Usually hidden in the deepest part of the forest, it turns to let Baba Yaga enter when she recites an incantation: "Little hut, little hut, turn your back to the forest and your front to me."

The hut on fowl's legs is brought to life in the penultimate movement of Mussorgsky's suite through music that will give you goose bumps!

Pictures at an Exhibition is a suite of 15 pieces composed for the piano. However, the version for orchestra by French composer Maurice Ravel is probably better known. Mussorgsky composed the piece as a tribute to the artist and architect Viktor Alexandrovich Hartmann, a close friend, who died at the age of 39. The inspiration for the work comes from a posthumous exhibition of ten of Hartmann's paintings, which the composer depicted in music. The suite begins with a promenade portraying a visitor strolling through the exhibition. This theme is interjected between various movements throughout the composition, each time transformed to reflect the impressions left on the spectator by the last painting.

7 The Gnome

Pictures at an Exhibition (Modest Mussorgsky)
Orchestral suite

In Northern European mythology, gnomes are small supernatural beings that live in the bowels of the earth, working in mines and guarding underground treasures, such as jewels and precious metals. Originally, gnomes were considered generous, albeit somewhat mischievous and quite ugly. Over time, they came to be seen as wicked.

One of Hartmann's paintings depicts a Christmas decoration in the form of a gnome with twisted legs. It served as Mussorgsky's inspiration for the first movement following the introductory Promenade and exploits dissonance to create an image of a deformed and repugnant creature.

8 In the Hall of the Mountain King

Peer Gynt (Edvard Grieg)
Orchestral suite

The Mountain King who appears in the play *Peer Gynt* is none other than the King of the Trolls, imaginary creatures of Scandinavian mythology often depicted as boorish, malicious, ugly creatures living in caves.

Peer Gynt is the story of an egotistical and ambitious young man who travels the world in search of wealth and pleasure. When he returns to his native village after 20 years of wandering, he discovers on his deathbed that the happiness he sought had been hiding there all the time.

In the Hall of the Mountain King describes one of Peer Gynt's adventures. He enters the kingdom of the trolls to seduce the King's daughter. After achieving his purpose, he secretly decides to flee the cave and its bloodthirsty denizens.

Written in verse, Henrik Ibsen's play was presented for the first time in 1876 in Oslo, accompanied by Grieg's music. When the first performances proved enormously successful, Grieg decided to transform the original score into two orchestral suites so that the music could be performed on its own.

Der Erlkönig (The Elf King)

9

Der Erlkönig (Franz Schubert)
Lied for voice and piano

Elves are magical creatures of Norse mythology who live in remote areas such as forests and caves. Their name means "white, clear and luminous," and they are portrayed as men and women of great beauty. Although elves were originally seen as kind, over time they came to be feared. According to German and Danish folklore, the appearance of the Elf King foretold imminent death.

Der Erlkönig tells the story of a father carrying his ill son home on horseback through a storm in the dark of night. The fear-stricken child describes the appearance of a fantastic creature to his father.

Who rides at this late hour through night and wind?
It is the father with his child;
He holds the boy well in his arm,
He grasps him safely, he keeps him warm.

"My son, why do you hide your face in fear?"
"Do you not see, my father, the Elf King?
The Elf King with crown and train?"
"My son, it is a streak of fog."

"My dear child, come along with me!
I am going to play nice games with you;
Many lovely flowers grow by the shore,
My mother has many golden clothes."

"My father, my father, do you not hear,
What the Elf King is promising me in a low voice?"
"Be quiet, stay quiet, my child:
It is the wind whispering in the dry leaves."

"Will you not go with me, dear boy?
My daughters will take good care of you;
My daughters lead the nightly round
And sway and dance and sing with you."

"My father, my father, do you not see over there
The daughters of the Elf King in that gloomy place?"
"My son, my son, I can see it well,
The old willows there are looking so gray."

"I love you, your beautiful shape appeals to me,
You either agree or I will use force."
"My father, my father, how he is touching me!
The Elf King has done great harm to me."

The father is frightened, he rides very fast,
In his arms he holds the moaning child.
He barely manages to reach his home.
In his arms the child... was dead.

10 Danse Macabre

Danse Macabre (Camille Saint-Saëns)
For orchestra

The imaginary creatures featured in this work are nothing less than skeletons risen from the grave to perform a peculiar dance.

In composing the music, Camille Saint-Saëns was inspired by Henri Cazalis' poem *La danse macabre,* itself based on a medieval tradition.

The interminable wars, famines and plagues that ravaged fifteenth-century Europe traumatized people with omnipresent death, reducing the population by half. This was when the *danse macabre,* or dance of death, first appeared in art, literature and theatre in the form of a rondo in which the dead danced with the living—rich and poor alike, young and old—to convey the notion that whatever one's station in life, all succumb to death.

No need to be frightened by the sinister theme of the dance, though—it's actually quite fun!

11 Dance of Terror

Love, the Magician (Manuel de Falla)
Ballet

In many cultures, ghosts, or phantoms, are the spirits of the deceased that have once again assumed human form to return among the living.

Love, the Magician tells the story of the young Candelas, a beautiful gypsy tormented by the ghost of her deceased fiancé. She decides to invoke a series of curses and spells to rid herself of these apparitions, which are impeding the course of her love for Carmelo. In the *Dance of Terror*, which occurs towards the beginning of the ballet, Candelas is caught between horror and fascination as she dances with her fiancé's ghost, who is as possessive in death as he was in life.

Manuel de Falla drew on legends of witchcraft and Andalusian gypsy music in composing his ballet *Love, the Magician*.

12 Dance of the Blessed Spirits

Orpheus and Eurydice (Christoph Willibald Gluck)
Instrumental interlude

The blessed spirits are the souls of the righteous, who, upon dying,
would go to a special place in the Underworld that the ancient Greeks called
the Elysian Fields.

Unlike many other tales, this is not a story of the dead returning to our world,
but rather of a living person (Orpheus) who visits the Kingdom of the Dead
to seek his beloved, Eurydice.

The opera *Orpheus and Eurydice* is based on the story of their love. In Greek
mythology, Orpheus is an extraordinary musician who loses his sweet Eurydice
when she is bitten by a snake. Through his singing, the inconsolable Orpheus is
able to move the spirits guarding the Kingdom of the Dead to allow him to enter
in search of his beloved. As he travels through the Underworld to reach the
Elysian Fields, we hear the *Dance of the Blessed Spirits,* an orchestral
selection from the opera so popular that it is often played on its own.

13 Ride of the Valkyries

The Valkyrie (Richard Wagner)
Instrumental prelude

In Norse mythology, the Valkyries are divine maidens serving the gods of war and represented as exceptionally beautiful golden-haired women. Riding winged horses, they wear helmets and bear spears. Their main mission is to gather the souls of valiant warriors who have died in combat and lead them to Valhalla, the Hall of the Gods.

The Valkyrie alluded to in the opera's title is Brünnhilde, the favourite daughter of the god Wotan. The two argue bitterly when she defends the courageous Siegmund.

This is one of four operas comprising the *The Ring of the Nibelung* cycle and the one most often performed. The most familiar excerpt from the opera is *The Ride of the Valkyries,* which is the prelude to the third and final act.

14 The Queen of the Night Aria

The Magic Flute (Wolfgang Amadeus Mozart)
Aria for voice and orchestra

The Queen of the Night does not look like a typical witch: she is a beautiful and powerful sorceress in *The Magic Flute,* who appears with a large cape depicting a starry night. The plot of this opera owes much to fairy tales. Tamino is a prince who has been given the task of saving the Queen of the Night's daughter, Princess Pamina, held prisoner in Sarastro's palace. Tamino undertakes his quest armed only with a magic flute.

At the beginning of the opera, we are led to believe that the Queen of the Night is a desperate mother whose daughter has been kidnapped. As the opera progresses, however, we gradually come to understand that, in reality, the wise priest Sarastro is holding Pamina in his palace to protect her against the influence of the evil Queen of the Night. When the Queen appears with a dagger in the second act to sing this superlative aria, any lingering doubt is removed. Her voice may bewitch, but her orders are clear: Pamina is to kill Sarastro with the dagger or she will no longer be the Queen's daughter.

15 Witches' Chorus

Macbeth (Giuseppe Verdi)
For choir and orchestra

Witches are usually flesh and blood creatures skilled in the art of sorcery, which gives them power over objects, animals and human beings. Some witches are able to see into the future.

In William Shakespeare's *Macbeth,* when three witches foretell that Macbeth will become king, his ambition for power is stirred. Perhaps for the sole reason that he believes in their prophesy, he abandons the role of loyal soldier to become an assassin. When Macbeth does finally become king as the witches predicted, he is loathed and eventually assassinated himself. Shakespeare's play was the main inspiration behind Giuseppe Verdi's most popular opera which he composed in 1847.

16 Witches' Dance

Witches' Dance (Niccolo Paganini)
Variations for violin and orchestra

For many centuries, it was believed that witches gathered to worship the devil. Known as "sabbats," their nocturnal assemblies were usually held in a remote forest clearing.

Tradition has it that a favourite site for these sabbats was the small Italian town of Benevento, where witches from all across Europe would gather to celebrate satanic rituals around a giant walnut tree.

Witches' Dance was inspired by *The Walnut Tree of Benevento,* a ballet by Franz Xaver Süssmayr, a disciple of Mozart. Paganini's music takes the form of a series of variations for violin and orchestra based on a melody from the ballet performed as the witches enter.

17 The Sorcerer's Apprentice

The Sorcerer's Apprentice (Paul Dukas)
Symphonic poem

Unlike other supernatural powers, sorcery can be learned. For this reason, various traditions hold that a young acolyte would learn magic formulas, spells and recipes for potions from an experienced sorcerer while serving as an apprentice.

In his ballad entitled *The Sorcerer's Apprentice,* German writer Johann Wolfgang von Goethe tells the story of a young initiate who brings a broom to life so that it can perform a task assigned by his master: fetching pails of water to fill a cistern. Everything seems to be going marvellously until the job is finished and the sorcerer's apprentice suddenly realizes he has no spell to stop the broom! In desperation, he shatters the broom, but this only makes matters worse—each fragment comes to life as a new broom, and they all set about fetching more and more water until the entire room is flooded. Finally, the master sorcerer returns and puts an end to the dire situation.

In 1897, Dukas composed a symphonic poem based on this legend that recounts the apprentice's woeful tale through a variety of musical resources, including rhythm, melody, and a rich spectrum of colours from the orchestra.

Walt Disney included an animated version of the piece in his classic 1940 film *Fantasia,* featuring Mickey Mouse as the young apprentice.

18 Devil's Trill Sonata

Devil's Trill Sonata (Giuseppe Tartini)
Sonata for violin and basso continuo

The main figure in this piece is the devil himself—the proclaimed enemy of God, also known as Satan. According to popular belief, the devil is also the god of sorcerers. He is traditionally depicted in red, with horns, a tail, goat hooves and carries a trident.

Tartini recounts that one night he dreamed of the devil offering him a pact: glory and fame in exchange for his soul. In turn, Tartini dared the devil to play the violin. To his great surprise, the devil divinely played the most beautiful music Tartini had ever heard. At that moment, he awoke in an impassioned state.

Tartini immediately picked up his violin, desperate to recreate some of what he had just heard, but to no avail. In his own words: "The music which I at this time composed is indeed the best that I ever wrote, and I still call it the *Devil's Trill,* but the difference between it and that which so moved me is so great that I would have destroyed my instrument and have bid farewell to music forever if it had been possible for me to live without the enjoyment it affords me."

The *Devil's Trill* is a sonata for violin and basso continuo composed by Tartini in the aftermath to this dream. While the composer claims that the entire sonata was inspired by the devil's music, the famous "devil's trill" do not appear until the third movement.

19 The Devil's Staircase (Étude N° 13)

Études (György Ligeti)
Étude for piano

It is universally held that the devil is ubiquitous. In this piece, he is even found in mathematics! *The Devil's Staircase* is a popular name for an infinitely rising mathematical function that challenges intuitions about continuity and measure. Ligeti had a lifelong interest in mathematics, and it would appear that he based *Étude No. 13* for piano on the graph of the Cantor function.

In the latter part of his life, Ligeti composed a magnificent series of études, which he claimed were to improve his own poor technique. In these studies, he strives to create acoustic illusions through rhythm and melody, not unlike the contradictory perspectives found in the drawings of Maurits Escher.

Sit back and enjoy this diabolical study!

20 Infernal Dance of All Kashchei's Subjects

The Firebird (Igor Stravinsky)
Suite from the ballet

In Slavic mythology, Kashchei is an immortal evil figure depicted as a hideous skeletal old man. His soul has been removed from his body and hidden in an egg within a duck within a hare within a chest buried beneath a tree on an island in the middle of the ocean. It is said that anyone who finds the egg and breaks it—a virtually impossible task given how well it is hidden —will destroy Kashchei.

The ballet version of *The Firebird* draws on several Russian folk tales. One night, the valiant Prince Ivan becomes lost in an enchanted forest while searching for a thief who has stolen golden apples from his father's garden. Suddenly, a firebird appears. Ivan is enthralled and chases the bird until he finally catches it. After forcing the firebird to make a pact in exchange for its freedom, the Prince meets a beautiful princess and falls in love. She must soon leave, but first warns the Prince that danger awaits if he does not leave the forest. Just then, Kashchei the Immortal appears with his demonic horde, and they perform this sinister infernal dance.

Listening Guide

1 The Fairy-Queen

The Fairy-Queen (Henry Purcell) ❋ Solo, Chorus and Dance of Fairies ❋ The Scholars Baroque Ensemble

In listening to the music, you will hear the clear timbre of the soprano singing a melody that seems to leap to and fro with its lightly syncopated rhythm. When the voices of the choir join in, the overall musical effect is one of lightness and well-being—exactly the mood the fairies hope to restore for their queen.

2 A Midsummer Night's Dream

A Midsummer Night's Dream (Felix Mendelssohn) ❋ Scherzo from the orchestral suite, Opus 61 ❋ Scottish Chamber Orchestra ❋ Conductor: Jaime Laredo

Listen to how quickly and lightly the notes are played in a strongly marked, regular rhythm typical of a scherzo. If you rapidly count 1, 2, 3; 1, 2, 3; 1, 2, 3 while emphasizing each "1," you will easily locate the beginning of each measure. As the music starts, you will also notice the delicate high sounds of the woodwinds rising above the accompaniment in the strings. Pay close attention to how the sound grows louder as more instruments join in. Among these, you will feel the rumbling strength of rolls played on the timpani.

3 Puck's Dance

Preludes (Claude Debussy) ❋ Prelude for piano, Book 1 ❋ Piano: Martin Jones

This piece for solo piano begins with a flippant theme with a playful rhythm based on a long note followed by a short one. The melody is repeated several times, as though it were gathering speed to take flight. After a number of unsuccessful attempts, the melody finally achieves its objective with a burst of energy that leads to a trill lasting for numerous measures before descending again. This cheerful music captures Puck's manner of suddenly appearing, disappearing or erupting into laughter.

4 Dance of the Sugar Plum Fairy

The Nutcracker (Pyotr Ilych Tchaikovsky) ❋ Ballet suite, Opus 71a ❋ Philharmonia Slavonica
❋ Conductor: Hans-Peter Gmür

At the beginning of the scene, the strings play a serene, almost imperceptible, rhythm that keeps us expectant
A sound like the tinkling of glass then appears; this is the celesta, a percussion instrument with a very unusual timbre
The slightly repetitive and hypnotic melody brings to mind the movement of a music box ballerina.

5 The Witch Baba Yaga

Album for the Young (Pyotr Ilych Tchaikovsky) ▨ For piano ▨ Piano: Idil Biret

This short piece begins with a musical motive comprising four notes. The first three are soft and quick, the fourth
accented. This way of accenting a musical phrase, known as anacrusis, is used by Tchaikovsky to portray the
inconspicuous appearance of the terrible witch Baba Yaga. All along the piece, which is quick and light throughout,
the motive of three similar rising notes and a fourth accented note is constantly repeated, creating a melody that is
predictable and fun.

Tchaikovsky may have used the anacrusis technique to echo the feelings of little children listening to tales of witches:
they are afraid, even though they know it is just a story.

6 — The Hut on Fowl's Legs

Pictures at an Exhibition, IX (Modest Mussorgsky) ❀ Orchestral suite
❀ Radio Symphony Orchestra Moscow ❀ Conductor: Alexander Mikjailov

The movement begins with decisive chords played by all the strings in the low register, accompanied by the bass drum and timpani, immediately evoking the evil presence of the witch Baba Yaga, who lives in the hut on fowl's legs. Following the introduction's overwhelming atmosphere of terror, an accelerating rhythm is perhaps suggestive of the frenetic flight of an unfortunate victim attempting to flee the witch. Various instruments of the orchestra can be heard (the woodwinds join the strings, followed by the brass and then cymbals) as the action increases. In the slower, gentler middle section, the conspicuously reedy timbre of the bassoon—far from being reassuring—serves to further increase the suspense. This part concludes with some mysterious trills that announce a violent return of the chase in all its terror.

7 — The Gnome

Pictures at an Exhibition, I (Modest Mussorgsky) ❀ Orchestral suite
❀ Radio Symphony Orchestra Moscow ❀ Conductor: Alexander Mikjailov

The composer captures our attention from the outset with a loud, abrupt motive. A fragmented musical dialogue follows, full of repetitions, interruptions and threatening silences that caricature the clumsy movements of the gnome. Pay close attention to the various timbres of the percussion section and to the lower instruments of the orchestra.

8 — In the Hall of the Mountain King

Peer Gynt (Edvard Grieg) ▓ Orchestral suite, N°1, Opus 46 ▓ Philharmonia Slavonica
▓ Conductor: Alberto Lizzio

This movement, which depicts Peer Gynt tiptoeing out of the hall, begins with a soft note in the French horns. The strings then introduce a march-like rhythm (1, 2; 1, 2; 1, 2) that grows ever stronger, over which begins the famous melody (played by the bassoons and doubled by the cellos and double basses in pizzicato). The melody is repeated faster and faster throughout the piece, swelling in volume, with more instruments joining in as Peer is chased by the furious trolls. When they finally catch him, loud shots resound in the percussion section.

9 Der Erlkönig (The Elf King)

Der Erlkönig (Franz Schubert) ▪ Lied for voice and piano, D. 328 ▪ Baritone: Dietrich Fisher-Dieskau ▪ Piano: Gerald Moore

When listening to this piece, it is important to be aware that the singer assumes four different roles (the narrator, the father, the son and the Elf King) by giving each a unique vocal characterization. Even if you don't understand German, if you listen closely throughout the song, the music and intonation will let you know who is talking. The song starts with frantic and obsessive triplets in the piano imitating the hooves of a galloping horse. Over this incessant accompaniment, the neutral voice of the narrator enters to set the stage. Next, you will hear the voice of the father in a low register. The son's voice grows increasingly desperate, rising a tone (D, E, F) each time it enters with the anguished plea: *Mein Vater!* (My father!). Finally, the Elf King is portrayed by an undulating melody sung pianissimo to create an alluring and persuasive effect. In the final verse, the music accelerates (as the father presses the horse to ride even faster) until, suddenly, the accompaniment stops and the narrator confirms our worst fears: *das Kind war tot* (the child… was dead).

10 Danse Macabre

Danse Macabre (Camille Saint-Saëns) ❀ For orchestra ❀ CSR Symphony Orchestra (Bratislava) ❀ Conductor: Stephen Gunzenhauser

At the beginning of the piece, which is set in a cemetery, twelve soft notes sound midnight and death appears; a solo violin starts to play, and the dance begins. Pay close attention to the dissonance of the violin's first notes, which form the interval of a tritone, or three whole tones. Known in the Middle Ages as *diabolus in musica* ("the devil in music"), its use was strictly forbidden. The main theme of the dance now enters, played first by the flute and then picked up by the strings. The skeletons have risen from the grave and are dancing. Next, the violin of death introduces a new melody to a waltz rhythm. As more skeletons join the dance, the music begins to intensify until the two original melodies return, played by even more instruments. You will notice, however, that the solo violin continues to dominate. Finally, the skeletons dance so furiously that their bones begin to rattle, an effect produced by the xylophone.

11 Dance of Terror

Love, the Magician (Manuel de Falla) ◉ Ballet ◉ Ljubljana Radio Symphony Orchestra ◉ Conductor: Anton Nanut ◉ Mezzo-soprano: Eva Novsak-Houska

The appearance of the ghost is heralded by a trumpet in an insistent melody shaped from repeated notes played decrescendo. This is followed by a glissando that shivers up and down through the entire orchestra. Next, a marked rhythm lays a foundation for the first theme of the dance. Shortly thereafter, a new theme (as oppressive as the first through repetitions of a single motive on different levels) enters and then becomes interwoven with the first.

12 Dance of the Blessed Spirits

Orpheus and Eurydice (Christoph Willibald Gluck) ✤ Instrumental interlude ✤ Academy of Saint Martin in the Fields ✤ Conductor: Iona Brown

The excerpt included here is the middle section of the *Dance of the Blessed Spirits*. The clear sound of the flute seems to rise and float over a background of strings in a sublime melody that reflects the serenity of the blessed spirits while also conveying a certain melancholy.

13 Ride of the Valkyries

The Valkyrie (Richard Wagner) ✤ Instrumental prelude ✤ London Philharmonic Orchestra ✤ Conductor: Alberto Lizzio

This piece has been used frequently in advertising, films and videos, for it powerfully evokes a sense of impending importance. Listen carefully to how this is achieved by linking two musical elements: the initial motive—primarily in the strings and high winds—rises with breathtaking speed and is repeated nine times beginning on different notes. The exciting rhythm of galloping, in a slightly lower register, begins almost imperceptibly with the fifth statement of the motive, gradually taking over as the main theme. It finally imposes its presence when played fortissimo by the brass instruments.

14 The Queen of the Night Aria

The Magic Flute (Wolfgang Amadeus Mozart) ✤ Aria for voice and orchestra, KV 620 ✤ Budapest Failoni Chamber Orchestra ✤ Conductor: Michael Halasz ✤ Soprano: Hellen Kwon

The voice of the soprano singing this soaring melody with its flood of high notes is dazzlingly beautiful. When we listen to her words, however; we realize that Mozart's music deliberately expresses the Queen of the Night's anger and unquenchable thirst for vengeance.

Hell's vengeance
boils in my heart;
Death and despair
blaze around me!

If Sarastro does not feel the pain
of death because of you,
Then you will be my daughter nevermore.

15 Witches' Chorus

Macbeth (Giuseppe Verdi) ❀ For choir and orchestra ❀ Orchestra e Coro del Teatro alla Scala

This excerpt is the first encounter with the witches. In several ways, Verdi's characterization of them reveals the ambivalence of his feelings for them. At the beginning, the low strings are juxtaposed with the high winds in an idea that is repeated three times. The entire orchestra then plays a variation of this theme, the low part instilling terror and the upper voices suggesting the witches' devious intentions. Next, we hear the witches' first words, spoken more than sung. At first, they seem menacing, but a change in rhythm leads to a mocking melody.

16 Witches' Dance

Witches' Dance (Niccolo Paganini) ❀ Variations for violin and orchestra ❀ London Philharmonic Orchestra ❀ Conductor: Charles Dutoit ❀ Violin: Salvatore Accardo

In this excerpt from the middle of the piece, the orchestra remains in the background while the soloist takes centre stage. After the violin has played the main melody, the virtuosic resources of this superb instrument are showcased: double and triple stops (two or three notes played simultaneously), pizzicato (the characteristic sound of strings plucked by a finger) and harmonics (extremely high notes with an eerie quality).

17 The Sorcerer's Apprentice

The Sorcerer's Apprentice (Paul Dukas) ❀ Symphonic poem ❀ CSR Symphony Orchestra (Bratislava) ❀ Conductor: Kenneth Jean

If you listen closely, you will hear the music depict the exact moment the enchanted broom comes to life. After a short silence, a walking rhythm begins. This serves as the backdrop for a melody in the bassoons, with their characteristic timbre, depicting the broom's short steps as it carries buckets of water. Some wind instruments now enter in support of the theme. If you pay attention, you will notice brief interruptions by the violins representing water being poured. Shortly thereafter, the imposing sound of the trumpet accentuates the broom's theme even more, followed by a lovely melody in some high instruments (notably the xylophone and the piccolo) conveying the apprentice's satisfaction at the success of his spell. We know the situation has taken a turn for the worse when the broom theme returns with a crescendo through the entire orchestra.

18 Devil's Trill Sonata

Devil's Trill Sonata (Giuseppe Tartini) ✤ Sonata for violin and basso continuo
✤ Violin: Anne-Sophie Mitter

n this excerpt, the violin plays an energetic and dramatic theme. An ensemble of strings and piano provide the accompaniment and dialogue with the soloist. Listen closely and you will hear the violin begin a trill and then, as the trill continues, start a new melody on other strings. This technical feat lasts for several measures. The tension builds until he passage suddenly ends and the violin turns to a melody showcasing the instrument's unique expressive qualities.

19 The Devil's Staircase (Étude N° 13)

Études (György Ligeti) ✤ Étude for piano N°13 ✤ Piano: Erika Haase

Starting in the lowest register of the piano, the music madly begins to rise with a throbbing rhythm through every note of the keyboard, as though it were fleeing the depths of hell. Every time the music reaches notes in the upper register, where a point of escape might be within sight, the devil gains the upper hand and the pattern begins again.

20 Infernal Dance of All Kashchei's Subjects

The Firebird (Igor Stravinsky) ✤ Suite from the ballet ✤ London Philharmonic Orchestra
✤ Director: Robert Craft

The piece begins with a short and powerful chord played fortissimo by the full orchestra, catching both the audience and Prince Ivan by surprise and announcing the sudden appearance of King Kashchei. (This abrupt chord reappears several times at the whim of the powerful Kashchei, like the snap of a whip that accentuates, interrupts or pushes aside the melody.) Kashchei's theme now begins, played by wind instruments in a low register to evoke the wizard's dark nature. You will notice a growing feeling of dread created by the syncopated rhythm of the melody as it rejects traditional rules of musical accentuation.

Listen closely to the way this stunning composition employs just the right musical effects to bring to life the action on the stage: the pursuit and capture of Ivan, the ritual dance to turn him into stone, and the miraculous appearance of the firebird that breaks the spell at the last moment. The music is breathtaking from start to finish.

The Composers

Henry Purcell (1659–1695)

Born in Wesminster to a family of musicians, Purcell is considered to be one of the finest English composers of all time. He began singing in the Chapel Royal at the age of 10, then became assistant to the keeper of the King's instruments when his voice changed.

When he was 18, Purcell was named composer-in-ordinary for the King's Violins. He was later appointed organist of Westminster Abbey and then of the Chapel Royal. In addition to music for theatres, the church and amateur musicians, Purcell also taught music to members of the aristocracy and composed several odes and ceremonial hymns for special court occasions.

His works combine French and Italian Baroque elements with traditional English musical forms. Purcell died in London on November 21, 1695, at the height of his popularity. His body lies beneath the organ in Westminster Abbey, where he served as organist for so many years. His epitaph reads: "Here lyes Henry Purcell, Esq., who left this life and is gone to that blessed place where only his harmony can be exceeded."

Felix Mendelssohn (1809–1847)

Born in Hamburg, Mendelssohn was the son of a banker and nephew to a famous philosopher. As a child prodigy, he quickly displayed exceptional talent for music, drawing, and literature— gifts that his family valued and encouraged. The young Felix began studying piano with his mother and composition with Carl Friedrich Zelter. At the age of 14, Mendelssohn had access to a private orchestra, which inspired him to write even more music. He directed the orchestra in performances of his own compositions in the family garden before friends and relatives. He began to dedicate his life to music, making concert tours across Europe, working as a conductor in several German cities and supporting the creation of new schools of music, including the Leipzig Conservatory. In addition to working tirelessly as a pianist, conductor and teacher, Mendelssohn was also a prolific composer. His works include symphonies, concertos, oratorios, overtures, piano pieces and chamber music. He died at the young age of 38.

Claude Debussy (1862–1918)

Debussy was raised in a family of modest means living near Paris. He was soon noticed for his quick intelligence and remarkable musical talent, which earned him a place at the Paris Conservatoire at just 10 years of age. Some time later during his studies, he had an opportunity to travel to Florence, Venice, Vienna and Moscow as a music teacher to the children of an aristocratic family, an experience that enriched his musical education. The young composer began to develop a reputation as a nonconformist who disregarded formal rules in favour of an unusual intuition in matters of harmony. This trait antagonized the more traditional teachers at the conservatory. Nevertheless, in 1884, he was awarded the prestigious Prix de Rome—the institution's highest honour, comprising a scholarship for the winner to study for two years at the Villa Medici in the Italian capital. When the scholarship ended, Debussy took up permanent residence in Paris, where he dedicated his life to composing.

Debussy's ability to evoke landscapes, sounds and atmospheres through his music led to his being associated with the Symbolist poets and Impressionist painters. Like them, he was interested in quick changes of colour and intensity and had a taste for subtle nuance. Although his music is often described as Impressionist, even today, Debussy did not found a school of composition by that name; he simply freed music from its traditional harmonic limits. His works provide proof that experimentation can lead to new ideas and techniques.

Pyotr Ilyich Tchaikovsky (1840–1893)

One of the most celebrated composers of the romantic period. Tchaikovsky defined his work as the "musical confession of the soul."

From a very young age, Tchaikovsky was emotional and sensitive, earning him the nickname "porcelain child." He had a particular talent for music and, when he learned to play the piano, he would concentrate so hard when playing the instrument that he would end up exhausted, nervous and unable to sleep.

Out of family obligation, Tchaikovsky studied law and became a lawyer. However, at the age of 22, he decided to devote himself entirely to music and enrolled in the Saint Petersburg Conservatory. To earn a living, he taught piano and music theory. In 1885, Tchaikovsky's fame grew to soaring heights in Russia and the rest of Europe, before crossing the Atlantic to reach the United States. In 1890, he was invited to inaugurate Carnegie Hall in New York and, in 1893, was voted a member of the Académie des Beaux- Arts de l'Institut de France and obtained an honorary doctorate from the University of Cambridge.

Among his vast body of work, ever expressive and seductive, the three most famous are the three ballets, *Swan Lake, Sleeping Beauty* and *The Nutcracker.*

Modest Mussorgsky (1839–1881)

A unique and influential Russian Nationalist composer of the 19th century. Mussorgsky lived on his parents' farm until the age of 10. His childhood left a lasting impression on him, and the composer soaked up all the sensibility and humour of the people in his village.

Later on, in his musical body of work, he reproduced elements of Russian popular culture that had made such an impression on him as a child. It was his mother who taught him to play the piano, and he continued with excellent private teachers. Despite his musical vocation, Mussorgsky entered the Cadet School of the Guards of Saint-Petersburg to pursue a military career. At 18, he met the Russian Nationalist composers with whom he would form the group known as The Five. In 1858, he abandoned his military career to devote himself entirely to music, but in 1863, he was forced to take an administrative job to support himself.

Mussorgsky was a self-taught composer. His bold and unorthodox harmonies, inspired by the repertoire of Russian folk music, influenced other foreign composers. His songs and operas reflected the desire to emulate the rhythms and tones of the Russian language.

Edvard Grieg (1843–1907)

Grieg studied piano with his mother, a professional pianist, before entering the conservatory in Leipzig, Germany. Following his studies, for three years he remained in Copenhagen, the heart of Scandinavian cultural life at the time.

In 1867, Grieg moved to Oslo, where he founded the Norwegian Academy of Music. In addition to his career as a pianist, he conducted orchestras and choirs and taught composition. During his many concert tours, he met leading composers, such as Liszt, Tchaikovsky, Brahms and Wagner, and also had the opportunity to present his own compositions—thereby introducing Norwegian music to all of Europe. In 1874, the government awarded Grieg an annual pension so that he could dedicate himself completely to composing. His works, which are strongly influenced by Norwegian folk music, have an attractive simplicity combined with great harmonic originality.

Franz Schubert (1797–1828)

Born in Vienna, Schubert was the 12th of 14 children of a modest schoolmaster. At the age of five, he began taking piano, violin and singing lessons; his teachers were stunned by the ease with which he learned to play at such a young age. Schubert, who passed away at the tender age of 31, was one of the first composers of the romantic period. His talent grew in the shadow of Beethoven, whom he profoundly admired. It was only after his death that his art began to be recognized and to gain the admiration of critics and the public. Schubert passed away one year after Beethoven and, as per his final wishes, was buried next to him.

Schubert devoted much of his creative energy to lyrical song (*lied*), an immensely popular genre in the romantic period. A prominent German singer summarized the career of the Austrian composer as follows: "When song and poetry arrived on the earth, they were personified in Franz Schubert."

Camille Saint-Saëns (1835–1921)

An extremely talented musician, Saint-Saëns was a piano virtuoso, organist, conductor, music critic and composer, but also a multifaceted intellectual. In addition to being greatly involved in music, he was also interested in various other disciplines, including geology, archaeology, botany and entomology. A member of the Société Astronomique de France, he often planned his concerts to coincide with astronomical events.

His extensive work, which includes more than 400 compositions from almost every genre, was very eclectic, extremely classical and masterful but, at times, a little contrived. For this reason, he was deemed to be too academic. Saint-Saëns was the first renowned composer to compose music for a motion picture.

Manuel de Falla (1876–1946)

Born in Cádiz, Spain, de Falla studied piano first with his mother and grandfather and later with other teachers. It was not until the age of 17, however, when he attended the performance of a concerto, that he felt music to be his true calling. De Falla moved to Madrid when he was 20 to pursue professional studies. At 23, he received a degree from the Escuela Nacional de Música y Declamación, where he was unanimously awarded the first prize in piano. While in Madrid, he met and began studying composition with the prestigious musicologist Felipe Pedrell. Pedrell felt that a nation's music should be rooted in its folklore. Under the influence of his teacher, de Falla developed a distinctly nationalist style that marks almost all his compositions. He never borrowed folk melodies directly, however, choosing rather to draw on their spirit. From 1907 to 1914, de Falla lived in Paris, where he spent time with Claude Debussy and Maurice Ravel, whose influence can also be heard in his music. Upon returning to Spain, de Falla composed his most famous works. In 1939, following the Spanish Civil War, he went into exile in Argentina, where he died seven years later.

Christoph Willibald Gluck (1714–1787)

The son of a forest inspector, Gluck was introduced to music as a child by singing in his village church choir. He progressed quickly and soon learned to play several instruments. Receiving little support from his father, he left home at the age of 15 to travel the country, earning his living as a wandering musician before settling in Prague to study music more seriously. Following a European tour, he made his home in Vienna as the royal choir master in the court of Empress Maria Theresa. He was also music teacher to her children, including Marie-Antoinette, the future Queen of France.

Gluck's first operas were in the Italian style, marked by superficial splendour designed to showcase virtuoso singing. Over time, he developed a new, more restrained style intended to return opera to its original purpose: the expression of feelings and emotions through music.

Feeling misunderstood in Vienna, Gluck moved to Paris, where he could count on the support of Marie-Antoinette, his former pupil, and where the style of opera was more to his taste. An ideological clash subsequently erupted between partisans of the French tradition of reformed opera and advocates of Italian opera. After a few years, Gluck returned to Vienna where he lived out his remaining years as a virtual recluse.

Richard Wagner (1813–1883)

Born in Leipzig, Germany, Wagner was strongly influenced from a tender age by his stepfather—the actor, playwright and stage director Ludwig Geyer—, who shared with the young Richard a love of literature and the theatre. Upon discovering the works of Weber and Beethoven at the age of about 15, Wagner decided to dedicate himself to music, more specifically to opera—an art form that allowed him to explore several areas of interest simultaneously. His musical progress proved to be slow and painful, however, as he set about learning on his own. While struggling to get his compositions known, Wagner worked in regional theatres with extremely limited resources, where he performed various duties related to music. His 1843 opera *The Flying Dutchman,* followed by *Tannhäuser and Lohengrin,* began to reveal the extent of Wagner's dramatic and musical gifts. He used these gifts to undertake a complete renewal of opera, a process that would culminate with *Tristan and Isolde* and the four-opera cycle *The Ring of the Nibelung*. Wagner considered these operas to be "total works of art," bringing all artistic dimensions together in a unified whole. Wagner's musical innovations in the areas of melody, harmony and orchestration are so great that many theorists believe he forever changed the course of opera specifically and of composition in general.

King Ludwig II of Bavaria was one of Wagner's greatest admirers. With the king's support, Wagner was able to build the Bayreuth Festival Theatre dedicated exclusively to presenting his own works. The complexity of this theatre far exceeded the technical capacity of traditional opera halls.

Wolfgang Amadeus Mozart (1756–1791)

Austrian composer. He is the defining musician of the classical period, if not of all time.

At the age of three, Wolfgang Amadeus's favourite pastime was searching for, in his own words, "notes that love each other" on his father's clavichord. He began composing at the age of four, even before he could write. Wolfgang possessed exceptional talent, a will to learn and unmatched enthusiasm. His father, Leopold, himself an excellent musician, quickly realized that his son was a musical genius, and he abandoned his career as a violinist to devote himself entirely to Wolfgang's musical education. At the age of six, Wolfgang began making long trips in uncomfortable stagecoaches to perform concerts. His musical talent was acclaimed in the most powerful courts of Europe. It is estimated that, over the course of his life, Mozart spent 3,720 days travelling, which amounts to a total of 10 years! This is how Mozart spent his youth, establishing himself and gaining a solid musical culture and training that enriched his natural talent. However, the hoped-for wealth was not to be.

At the age of 26, Wolfgang settled in Vienna, the capital of Austria, to try his hand as an independent musician, something that was completely novel at the time. He would spend his adult life struggling to earn a living, teaching piano and producing commissioned compositions. Worn out by continuous musical production, disappointed by the lack of public response to his music and almost destitute, Mozart passed away on December 5, 1791, just before his 36th birthday.

He composed close to 600 works of extraordinary quality, in all the styles of his time.

Giuseppe Verdi (1813–1901)

Born into an Italian peasant family, Verdi began his musical studies in the town of Busseto, where he had the good fortune to meet Antonio Barezzi, a merchant and music enthusiast who would help finance his education. Just before turning 20, Verdi went to Milan to study at the conservatory, but was refused admission for "lack of talent." Refusing to be discouraged, he pursued his musical studies even more ardently.

The Milanese composer Vincenzo Lavigna took Verdi on as a student. Three years later, the successful debut of his first opera in Milan earned Verdi a contract with the prestigious La Scala opera house. Unfortunately, the subsequent failure of his second opera and, more importantly, the death of his wife and two children plunged him into a deep depression, and he considered abandoning his musical career altogether. One year later, however, the director of La Scala convinced Verdi to compose a new opera—*Nabucco*. This work had an enormous impact not only for its musical value but also for its subject: the slavery of the Jewish people exiled to Babylon. The Italian public saw the opera as an allegory for their own country's political situation. The ensuing success brought Verdi veneration and made him a symbol of the patriotic struggle to unify Italy.

Verdi transformed Italian opera, with its traditional plot lines and emphasis on vocal gymnastics whose sole purpose was to impress the public. His operas are remarkable for their emotional intensity, expressive melodies and dramatic characterizations.

Niccolo Paganini (1782–1840)

Born in Genoa, Paganini began learning the mandolin from his father when he was five. It is held that when the father recognized his son's extraordinary musical talent, the young prodigy was forced to practice for hours on end. He took up the violin two years later and, by the age of 14, had mastered the instrument. His instructors soon had to admit they had nothing more to teach him.

Starting in 1810, Paganini devoted 18 years of his life to performing concertos in every corner of the Italian peninsula. In 1828, he undertook a tour of Europe's leading cultural centres: Vienna, Prague, Warsaw and Berlin, followed by Paris and London. He was acclaimed the best violinist of his time, deemed capable of producing sounds never before heard from the instrument.

Paganini's virtuosic technique revolutionized violin playing while also bringing him glory and wealth. It was rumoured during his lifetime that his exceptional ability came from a pact with the devil. His unusual appearance did nothing to allay these rumours: a serious illness left him with the sallow complexion of a corpse which, instead of disgusting the public, added to his charismatic appeal.

While Paganini's technique had a powerful influence on succeeding generations of violinists, he had an even more lasting impact through his compositions, including the famous *24 Caprices for Solo Violin*. He was deeply admired by many composers, including Liszt, Chopin, Schumann and Brahms.

Paul Dukas (1865–1935)

Dukas began playing the piano at the age of five, and, by 14, he was already composing to pass the time during a period of convalescence. He went on to study harmony at the Paris Conservatoire.

A meticulous and perfectionist composer, Dukas wrote few pieces, but his music is always intriguing and very personal in style. Composing for him was always preceded by a long period of silence and meditation. His broad culture, intelligence and sound judgment were part of what made Dukas a brilliant music critic.

Despite the phenomenal success of works such as the symphonic poem *The Sorcerer's Apprentice,* Dukas remained indifferent to honour, choosing to live a simple, discreet life away from the public eye. Deeply self-critical, he destroyed most of his compositions shortly before his death.

Giuseppe Tartini (1692–1770)

Destined from a young age to be a cleric, Tartini was enrolled at the University of Padua to study law. At the age of 18, however, he abandoned his call and married in secret after his father died. The ire of religious authorities at the university was raised when they learned of the marriage, and Tartini was exiled to the monastery in Assisi; there he studied violin and composition for three years. In 1716, he moved to Venice, where he is said to have heard the violinist Veracini. Deeply impressed and determined to learn to play as well, he locked himself away for four years in another monastery to master the violin. In 1721, he was named first violin at Basilica di Sant'Antonio in Padua and began a series of long and successful tours playing concertos abroad and teaching. Tartini founded a violin school that soon attracted students from across Europe. In addition to his violin compositions, Tartini wrote substantial treatises on the theory of music and acoustics.

György Ligeti (1923–2006)

Ligeti was born in Transylvania into a Hungarian family of Jewish origin. He claimed that the only musical instrument found in his home was a phonograph, and so he immersed himself in recordings. When he was 14, he convinced his parents that he should have piano lessons and, a year later, he was able to rent an instrument. At the age of 18, he entered the conservatory, but, at 21, as the Second World War raged, he was deported to a concentration camp by the Nazis. When the war ended, he resumed his music studies and, in 1949, graduated from the Franz Liszt Academy of Music in Budapest. He then taught at the academy and composed for six years until he emigrated to Vienna in 1956 for political reasons.

In Vienna, Ligeti developed a unique personal style that places greater emphasis on musical texture and colour than on melody and traditional harmony. A strong commitment to innovation is one of the main characteristics of his music. He explained that each of his works was the culmination of extensive exploration and, in turn, served as the starting point for a new musical quest. Much like Debussy in his time, Ligeti challenged existing ways of enjoying music by inviting listeners to approach it from a totally new perspective. When he died at the age of 83, Ligeti was already an acknowledged musical pioneer of the second half of the 20th century and considered one of the period's best composers. He is one of only a few contemporary composers whose music is frequently played and appreciated throughout the world.

Director Stanley Kubrick used Ligeti's music in his films 2001: *A Space Odyssey, The Shining and Eyes Wide Shut.*

Igor Stravinsky (1882–1971)

Russian composer who became a naturalized French citizen in 1936 and naturalized American citizen in 1945. A musical figurehead of the 20th century, he passed away just before his 89th birthday. This longevity allowed him to experience and create a wide range of musical trends and to distinguish himself in every style.

After obtaining his law degree in 1905, Stravinsky studied composition for five years with Nicolaï Rimski-Korsakov, then director of the Saint Petersburg Conservatory. Stravinsky's first compositions sparked the interest of Sergei Diaghilev, director of the Ballets Russes (a ballet company that aimed to showcase the cultural richness of Russia to all of Europe), who commissioned the score for *The Firebird*. In the years that followed, he continued his collaboration with Diaghilev, first composing the ballet *Petrushka* (1911) and then *The Rite of Spring* (1913), whose originality and primitive force caused a scandal at the premier. The intense dissonance and strong asymmetrical rhythms created such an uproar in the audience that the dancers could not even hear the orchestra. Shortly thereafter, however, the work enjoyed international acclaim. Despite the success of these three ballets, Stravinsky abandoned the Russian Nationalist style to take on new challenges. Upon his passing, which occurred almost 60 years later in the United States, Stravinsky left behind a large number of works of all genres: ballets, operas, symphonies, concertos and sonatas, in all musical styles. As per his last wishes, he was buried in Venice, near his old friend Sergei Diaghilev.

Glossary of Musical Terms

Accompaniment: A musical background in support of a melody.

Anacrusis: One or more unaccented notes occurring on the weak beat preceding the accented first beat of the following measure.

Aria: An operatic work for solo voice, usually accompanied by orchestra.

Ballet: A musical composition intended to accompany a staged dance performance.

Bass drum: A large drum with a low sound produced by beating the instrument with a mallet.

Basso continuo (or figured bass): A chord-based accompaniment system common during the Baroque period. Composers would write figures above notes of a bass line to indicate which chords performers were to improvise. The accompaniment was usually played on a harpsichord, organ or lute. Today, the piano often replaces the harpsichord.

Bassoon: A woodwind instrument in the double-reed family considered the bass version of the oboe.

Brass: A family of resonant wind instruments that includes the trumpet, the French horn, the trombone and the tuba.

Celesta: An instrument with a keyboard like that of a piano but whose sound is produced by hammers striking metal bars rather than strings. When struck, the bars vibrate causing a wooden box to resonate with a very soft and beautiful sound.

Cello: A string instrument of the violin family whose size and register lie between those of the viola and the double bass. The cello is held between the knees and the strings are played with a bow. Many consider it to be the string instrument that most closely resembles the human voice. The cello has been a popular instrument with composers throughout music history because of its warm tone, versatility and expressive qualities.

Choir: See Chorus.

Chord: The simultaneous sounding of three or more notes to produce a certain harmonic colour.

Chorus (or choir): An ensemble of singers performing a musical composition.

Concerto: A type of composition that appeared during the Baroque period in which a solo instrument is juxtaposed with a group of instruments (the orchestra). The solo instrument (the soloist) is featured while the orchestra plays an accompaniment role.

Crescendo: A gradual increase in volume achieved by playing an instrument more loudly or by adding more instruments during a passage.

Dissonance: A harsh or unpleasant sound produced by two or more notes that creates tension.

Double and triple stops: Refers to the advanced technique of playing two or three strings at the same time in order to produce two or three notes simultaneously.

Double bass: The largest and lowest of the bowed string instruments.

Étude (or study): A short musical composition intended to help performers practice and master a technical difficulty on a particular instrument. Many études have been composed for the piano over the course of music history, but most are simply exercises for the fingers; only a few—such as Ligeti's études —truly stand out for their virtuosity and musical qualities.

Figured bass: See Basso continuo.

Flute: A wind instrument. The simple design of the flute suggests that it may be the oldest of musical instruments. In one form or another, the flute is found in almost every known culture.

Fortissimo: An Italian term meaning "very loud." It is used in music to indicate an intense sound.

Glissando (Italian term derived from the French *glisser,* to slide"): A rapid execution of a scale toward the highest note (ascending) or the lowest (descending). In keyboard instruments such as the piano, it is produced by sliding the back of the hand across the white keys.

Harmonic: Within the complex sound of a single note, a secondary sound of a higher frequency occurring simultaneously with the fundamental pitch of a lower frequency.

Harmony: According to the standard dictionary definition, harmony is "a pleasing or congruous arrangement of parts." In music, harmony refers to the consonance or dissonance produced by two or more notes played simultaneously. It is also the study of the structure and progression of chords.

Incidental music: Music composed to accompany a dramatic work.

Interlude: A short composition performed as an intermission between two acts of an opera or two theatrical performances.

Interval: The distance in pitch between two notes.

Kettledrum: See Timpani.

Lied (from the German *lied,* "song," *lieder* in the plural): A short vocal setting of a poem with piano accompaniment. Well suited to the expression of emotions, this genre derived from folk music flourished during the Romantic period. Usually quite short, the lied sacrifices virtuosity in favour of poetry by using melody and accompaniment to express the poem's meaning through music.

Masque (or semi-opera): A predominantly English dramatic form popular during the late 17th century and early 18th century in which most of the action is spoken but interrupted by musical scenes (singing, dance, instrumental pieces). The result was a diverse and entertaining show.

Measure: Rhythmic division of a musical piece into equal parts.

Motif: Short melodic or rhythmic idea that is the primary unit of a musical fragment.

Movement: One complete section (i.e. with a beginning and an end) of a composite work performed in succession with other such single pieces.

Musical accentuation: In music, as in spoken language, some sounds are louder than others. The first beat of a measure is usually the most strongly accented.

Note: A musical symbol that represents a sound. The term is often used for the sound itself.

Opera: A classical music genre that began in Italy during the late Renaissance and early Baroque periods (circa 1600). It is defined as "a theatrical piece put to music." The dialogue is sung and accompanied by an orchestra.

Orchestra: A large group of musicians playing together. The size of an orchestra depends on the repertoire it performs.

Overture: An instrumental composition that serves to introduce a larger work such as an opera by presenting the themes to follow. The overture to Mendelssohn's *A Midsummer Night's Dream* was the first truly independent overture intended for performance as a concert piece.

Phrase: A section of a melodic line forming a complete idea.

Pianissimo: The superlative of piano, a word of Latin origin meaning "soft." It is used in music to indicate the quietest sound possible.

Piano: A keyboard string instrument invented around 1700. Pressing a key causes a hammer to strike the corresponding string and produce a sound. The word piano is an abbreviation of *pianoforte* (from the Italian *piano,* "soft," and *forte,* "loud"), which refers to the piano's ability to produce sounds of different intensities depending on the force applied to the keys, something not possible with its predecessors (the harpsichord and the clavichord), which were incapable of dynamic nuance. The piano is the most significant instrument of Western music. In addition to the vast repertoire composed for the piano and its expressive potential (it can produce more notes simultaneously than any other instrument), the piano is invaluable for learning the basics of music and an irreplaceable tool in the composition process.

Piccolo (from the Italian *flauto piccolo,* "small flute"): The piccolo is a small flute and, like all flutes, a member of the wind family. It has the highest timbre of any orchestral instrument and can be heard above the full ensemble because of its penetrating sound, especially in the upper register.

Pizzicato (from the Italian *pellizcado,* "pinched"): A sound obtained by plucking the strings of a bowed instrument with one's fingers.

Prelude (from the Latin *praeludere,* "to play beforehand"): A short piece in free form used to introduce a longer, more complex work. Originally, musicians would improvise a prelude before a concert to check their tuning. During the Romantic period, the compositions of Frédéric Chopin established the prelude as an independent musical form, primarily for the piano.

Register: The range of a voice or instrument (from the lowest pitch to the highest). The term is also used to distinguish various sections of this range: low register, middle register, high register.

Rhythm: The distribution of notes and rests in time.

Roll: A continuous, sustained sound obtained by rapidly beating a percussion instrument such as a drum or timpani.

Rondo (round or circle dance): A musical form based on the repetition of a theme. In a rondo, the main theme (A) is repeated at least three times in alternation with contrasting themes or couplets. The structure of the rondo is, therefore, A B A C A.

Scale: A series of sounds produced in ascending or descending order. The most widely known scale is "do-re-mi-fa-so-la-ti-do."

Scherzo (from the Italian *scherzo,* "game" or "joke"): A piece (or movement of a larger work) in triple meter that is frequently light and quick. Towards the end of the 18th century, the scherzo began to replace the minuet as the typica third movement in larger works.

Score: A written transcript of the notes of a musical work.

Semi-opera: See Masque.

Solo: A vocal or instrumental passage sung or played by one musician.

Soloist: A musician or instrument assigned a solo role (also see concerto).

Sonata: A composition comprising three or four movements for one or two instruments. During the Baroque period, the term was used freely to differentiate short instrumental pieces from a cantata, which included singing.

Soprano: The highest human voice. Different types of soprano are categorized by their vocal characteristics, such as light, lyrical or dramatic.

Strings: A family of instruments that produce sounds from vibrating strings. In the context of an orchestra, the string section includes violins, violas, cellos and double basses.

Study: See Étude.

uite: An instrumental composition comprising a series of hort sections or movements. The suite first appeared in the 6th century as a collection of folk songs and dances, usually in he same key. Although these songs and dances were separate novements, they were arranged to create contrasts of tempo ast and slow) and mood (majestic, cheerful, etc.). Today, the uite is just a series of short pieces with a common theme. Composers have often arranged music from their operas and allets into suites for concert performance.

ymphonic poem: An orchestral composition depicting an xtramusical story, such as a literary work, through music.

yncopation, syncopated: A displaced rhythmic effect achieved y tying one note on a weak beat to the note on the following trong beat. This reverses the normal order of strong and veak beats.

heme: The main idea, usually a recognizable melody, on vhich a composition is based in whole or in part.

imbre: The sound quality that distinguishes two instruments r voices from one another, even when producing the ame note.

impani (or kettledrum): The most important percussion nstrument in the orchestra comprising a skin stretched over . hollow copper shell. The tension in the skin (and therefore he pitch) can be adjusted by screws or a pedal. Orchestral vorks usually call for two or three timpani, each assigned . different note.

one: See Whole tone.

rill: A melodic ornament performed by rapidly and regularly lternating two pitches a whole tone or semitone apart.

riplet: A rhythmic figure consisting of three equal notes olayed in place of two notes of equal value.

rumpet: A wind instrument made from a long metal tube of expanding diameter from the mouthpiece to the bell. The rumpet has a bright military sound and is equipped with efficient valves capable of fingering rapid passages.

Variations: A musical form that begins with a melody that is repeatedly modified throughout the piece. There are many ways to vary a melody, such as adding ornamental notes or varying the rhythm, accompaniment or orchestration. The melody may be so altered that close attention must be paid to recognize it.

Violin: The smallest member of the string family and one of the most popular instruments. Its beautiful tone and impressive richness of expression make the violin an ideal solo instrument that has been treasured by musicians and music lovers for centuries. Together with the larger and deeper sounding members of its family, it also plays a leading role at the heart of the orchestra. The violin is played by drawing a bow across its strings. It can also be played by plucking strings with a finger to produce a sound called pizzicato.

Dating back to 1550, the violin is a descendant of the larger and deeper sounding viol family (viola d'amore, viola da gamba). On the surface, the violin is one of the simplest of modern instruments, comprising only a varnished wood sound box, a long neck and four taut strings. Appearances can be deceiving, however: it actually takes some 70 pieces to build a violin!

Waltz (from the German *walzan,* "to turn"): A familiar dance in triple time.

Whole tone (or simply tone): The distance between two pitches of different frequency equal to two semitones—the smallest interval on a keyboard.

Wind instruments: A family of instruments that produce sounds when a musician blows into them. This large family comprises two groups: woodwinds (flute, oboe, clarinet and bassoon) and brass (trumpet, horn, trombone and tuba).

Woodwinds: A group of wind instruments that includes the flute, oboe, English horn, clarinet and bassoon. The other group of wind instruments is the brass, whose sound is louder and brighter.

Xylophone: A percussion instrument with wooden bars of differing lengths set out horizontally like a keyboard and struck with two or four mallets.

Timeline of composers and periods

	1650	1700	1750
Purcell (1659–1695)			
Tartini (1692–1770)			
Gluck (1714–1787)			
Mozart (1756–1791)			
Paganini (1782–1840)			
Schubert (1797–1828)			
Mendelssohn (1809–1847)			
Wagner (1813–1883)			
Verdi (1813–1901)			
Saint-Saëns (1835–1921)			
Mussorgsky (1839–1881)			
Tchaikovsky (1840–1893)			
Grieg (1843–1907)			
Debussy (1862–1918)			
Dukas (1865–1935)			
de Falla (1876–1946)			
Stravinsky (1882–1971)			
Ligeti (1923–2006)			
	Renaissance		Baro[c]

1800   1850   1900   1950   2000

Classical   20th century

Music selection and explanatory notes Ana Gerhard

Illustrations Claudia Legnazzi

Translation from Spanish to English Helène Roulston and David Lytle

for Service d'édition Guy Connolly

Graphic design Francisco Ibarra Meza and Stéphan Lorti

Copy editing Ruth Joseph

First published in Spanish as *Seres fantásticos - Introducción a la música de concierto*

© 2013 Ana Gerhard (text), © 2013 Claudia Legnazzi (illustrations)

© 2013 Editorial Océano S.L., Barcelona (Spain)

Master recordings under license from Grupo Eurogyc de México

Ⓚ www.thesecretmountain.com

ⒸⓅ 2014 The Secret Mountain

ISBN-10: 2-924217-21-0 / ISBN-13: 978-2-924217-21-4